The Pomegranate Seeds

A CLASSIC GREEK MYTH

The Pomegranate Seeds

A CLASSIC GREEK MYTH

RETOLD BY LAURA GERINGER

ILLUSTRATED BY LEONID GORE

HOUGHTON MIFFLIN COMPANY

BOSTON · NEW YORK

1995

For information about this and other Houghton Mifflin trade and reference
books and multimedia products, visit The Bookstore at Houghton Mifflin
on the World Wide Web at (http://www.hmco.com/trade/).

Manufactured in the United States of America

Book design by David Saylor
The text of this book is set in 15½-point Monotype Fournier.
The illustrations are ink and acrylic, reproduced in full color.

HOR 10 9 8 7 6 5 4 3 2 1

Library of Congress Cataloging-in-Publication Data
Geringer, Laura.
The pomegranate seeds / by Laura Geringer ;
illustrated by Leonid Gore ; adapted from the tale by Nathaniel Hawthorne.
p.   cm.   ISBN 0-395-68192-8
1. Persephone (Greek deity)—Juvenile literature.
I. Gore, Leonid. II. Hawthorne, Nathaniel, 1804-1864. Tanglewood tales.
III. Title.   BL820.P7G47   1995
398. 21—dc20   94-11772   CIP   AC

For Adam, with love in all seasons
LAURA GERINGER

To Jenny

LEONID GORE

AUTHOR'S NOTE

I was drawn to this Greek myth because it celebrates the strength and determination of a mother who carries the torch for her child, as well as the resourcefulness of the child.

My retelling is inspired by Nathaniel Hawthorne's "Pomegranate Seeds," published in *Tanglewood Tales* in 1853, which emphasizes the coming-of-age theme and underplays Persephone's kidnapping. Hades is representative of life's darker side, but he is not evil. My Persephone is a more modern and outspoken girl than Hawthorne's. And like a present-day working mother, Demeter, though conflicted about leaving her daughter, must tend to her job. From other sources, I added the lizard boy. The boy is disrespectful to a goddess, but certainly does not deserve to die. I let him exact his own childish revenge so that Demeter's act of cruelty does not go unpunished.

I think Hawthorne would have approved of my bringing his tale into the 1990s. As he noted in his preface, "these immortal fables . . . are legitimate subjects for every age to clothe with its . . . manners and sentiment and to imbue with its own morality."

The Pomegranate Seeds

A CLASSIC GREEK MYTH

Demeter was very fond of her daughter, Persephone, so fond that she never let the girl out of her sight. It was harvest time, and the good goddess was very busy taking care of the crops all over the earth.

Putting a wreath of poppies on her head, she told her daughter to hurry. But Persephone did not want to hurry that morning.

"Why don't you go yourself today, Mother?" asked the girl. "I'll stay here and play in the ocean with the sea nymphs."

Demeter shook her head. "I need your help, Persephone," she said. "We'll take your pots of paint and you may put new stripes on any flower you choose. Quickly now, the sun will not wait."

"Please, Mother," Persephone pleaded. "I'm almost grown. Won't you let me stay by myself this once?"

Demeter sighed. She had been told many times by Zeus, king of the gods, that she protected her daughter too much. And her brother King Hades thought she should give the girl more freedom.

"You don't let her breathe," he had observed during one of his rare visits. But what would he know about breathing, living as he did down in the dark underworld with the spirits of the dead? And what would he know about raising a daughter when he loved only his jewels?

Demeter sighed again, more deeply this time. "You may stay with the nymphs then, Persephone," she said. "But take care not to go wandering in the fields by yourself."

Persephone promised and, by the time her mother's chariot had whirled out of sight, she was on the shore, calling the sea nymphs to rise out of the waves. They knew Persephone's voice, and it was not long before they showed their glistening faces and sea-green hair above the water. Sitting down on a bank of soft sponge, where the surf broke over them, they made a necklace of many-colored shells, which they hung around Persephone's neck.

"Let me run and gather flowers," said Persephone, "and I'll make a wreath as pretty as this necklace."

So Persephone left her friends and ran to the place where, only the day before, she had seen flowers. But they were now a little past full bloom so, not thinking of her promise to her mother, she wandered far into the fields.

Persephone had never seen such beautiful flowers: violets, roses, hyacinths, and pinks. She filled her apron and was turning back when she noticed a large bush covered with blood-red berries.

"How strange," she thought. "I was looking at that spot only a moment ago." She could not help thinking that it had suddenly sprouted out of the earth just to tempt her a few steps farther.

The plant bore more than a hundred ripe round berries. It was so unusual, she thought that she would try to pull it up and plant it in her mother's garden.

Laying down her flowers, Persephone seized the shrub and

pulled, but the soil stayed firm. Again, the girl pulled with all her might, and this time the earth began to stir and crack. There was a rumbling right beneath her feet. Did the roots go down into some enchanted cavern? She gave one last grand tug. Up came the bush, which moment by moment seemed to be growing larger. Persephone staggered back, gazing into the deep hole it had left in the earth.

The hole grew deeper and wider, until it seemed to have no bottom. And Persephone again heard a rumbling, which grew louder and nearer. It sounded like the tramp of hooves and the rattle of wheels.

Too frightened to run, Persephone soon saw a team of four black horses snorting smoke and tearing their way out of the earth. Tossing their black manes, the horses leaped out of the pit, pulling a splendid golden chariot. And in the chariot sat a man in black armor wearing a crown studded with diamonds. He kept rubbing his eyes and shading them with his hand, as if he did not like the sun.

The man beckoned to Persephone. "Don't be afraid," he said,

with a smile. "Do you remember me? I'm your uncle Hades. Come! Ride a little way with me."

But Persephone did not remember him and, in spite of his smile, he did not look very good-natured.

"Mother!" cried Persephone, alarmed. "Come quickly!"

But Demeter was at least a thousand miles away, making the corn grow in a distant country.

King Hades leaped to the ground, caught the girl in his strong arms, and, mounting the chariot, whipped the horses until they broke into so swift a gallop they seemed to be flying through the air. In an instant, Persephone lost sight of the pleasant Vale of Enna, where she had been born. Even the summit of Mount Etna had become so blue in the distance that she could scarcely distinguish it from the smoke that rose out of its crater.

"Your mother must have told you about me," said King Hades. "I am king of the underworld. Every flake of gold, every ounce of silver that lies under the earth belongs to me. You'll find me nicer than you think, once we get out of this disagreeable sunshine."

But Persephone would not stop wailing, for her mother *had* told her about her uncle Hades and his dark kingdom under the earth.

"Let me go home, oh let me go home!" she cried.

"My home is much grander than your mother's," answered King Hades. "Wait until you see my palace. If you like flowers, my little princess, I will give you flowers made of precious gems: pearls and diamonds and rubies."

"I don't care for gems," cried Persephone. "And I'm not your little princess."

King Hades frowned. "My palace needs a lively little girl to run upstairs and down, and brighten the rooms with her smile," he said.

"Never!" said Persephone. "I will never smile until you take me home."

But she might as well have been talking to the wind that whistled past, for Hades whipped his horses to go even faster. Persephone screamed so hard and so long that her voice almost disappeared. And when it was nothing but a whisper, she happened to glance over at a great broad field of golden grain, and saw her mother! Demeter was too busy making the corn grow to notice the golden chariot as it went hurtling along. The girl gathered all her strength and gave one last cry, but the chariot sped by before Demeter had time to turn her head.

King Hades had taken a road bordered with stony ravines and cliffs. Thick, twisted trees grew in the crevices of the rocks and, although it was barely noon, the air turned gray with twilight.

"Ah, what a relief to say good-bye to that awful glare," said the King. Persephone peered into his somber face in the gathering dusk.

"But I love the sun," she said. "Is there no sun at all in your kingdom?"

"None," said Hades proudly.

The horses plunged on into a grove of poplars so dense and dark, Persephone began to choke.

King Hades pointed triumphantly at the black gates looming up before them.

"Cerebus! Cerebus!" he cried, stopping the chariot "Come here, my good dog."

Persephone shuddered. The dog was a monster! He had three separate heads and when King Hades patted them all, he wagged his tail just like a sweet spaniel pup. But his tail was a live dragon, with fiery eyes and fangs!

"Don't be afraid," said her uncle. "He never hurts anyone unless they try to enter my kingdom without being invited. Or try to get away," he added, raising one eyebrow, "when I want to keep them here. Down, Cerebus! Now, dear Persephone, let's drive on."

Not far away from the gates, they came to an iron bridge, overhung by a giant cypress tree. The stream gliding beneath it was black and muddy. Its water reflected no images and it moved as slowly as if it had forgotten which way to flow.

"The River Lethe," observed King Hades, stopping the chariot again. "A single sip of its waters, and you will no longer miss your mother. In fact, you will forget your mother ever existed."

"Oh no!" cried Persephone. "I'd much rather be miserable

remembering my mother, than be happy having forgotten her." And she began to sob.

Taking Persephone by the hand, King Hades led her over the bridge and up a huge flight of steps to the entry hall of his towering palace. He ordered his servants to prepare a banquet and, above all, to remember to set a golden beaker of water from the River Lethe by Persephone's plate.

"I won't drink it," said Persephone, "and I won't eat any food, either. Your cook may just as well save himself the trouble, for I know the law. If once I taste the food of the dead, I'm yours forever."

Persephone was served beet soup with beet bread, red peppers, jam cake, red punch, and a tall tower of red jelly that, like a mirror, reflected her horrified face. Since her mother had never served such sweet and spicy things, the girl found it easy to shake her head and eat nothing that night, although she was very hungry.

Demeter, in the meantime, had mistaken the rattling of King Hades' chariot wheels for a peal of thunder. But the sound of

Persephone's cry startled her. She looked around in every direction, feeling certain that it was her daughter's voice. But how could the girl have traveled over so many lands and seas? Demeter tried to believe that it was the voice of another child, but the sound troubled her heart.

Mounting her chariot, she left the field in which she had been working and hurried home, only to discover that Persephone was gone. Demeter ran to the beach as fast as she could.

"Where is Persephone?" she demanded of the sea nymphs. "Where is my child?"

"Good mother," they called, "Persephone played with us, it's true; but she left long ago, meaning only to run a little way and gather some flowers for a wreath. And we haven't seen her since."

Demeter scarcely waited to hear more before hurrying off to search for her child. She knocked at the door of every cottage and farmhouse to ask if anyone had seen Persephone. The workers stood gaping at their doors, and invited her to come inside and rest.

At the door of every palace, she called so loudly that the servants hurried to throw open the gates, thinking it must be a great king or queen. When they saw only a sad woman with a wreath of poppies on her head, they spoke rudely and threatened to set the dogs on her.

At one fine house, a little gardener's helper was peeking out from behind a tool shed while the goddess greedily drank a goblet of water. The boy pointed his finger and laughed.

"Do you dare laugh at me in my grief?" she whispered hoarsely.

The rasping sound of her voice made him laugh all the louder. He slapped his knees and rolled in the dirt. But his mockery died, for, pointing at him, she whispered something under her breath and instantly the lad changed into a lizard with lidless eyes and no voice at all.

In a fury, Demeter swept away, and the unfortunate boy scuttled after her, maybe in the hopes that she would have mercy and change him back again. Perhaps she would have, too, for she was usually kind to children, but a hawk spotted him first and, swooping down, caught the lizard boy in its beak and flew away.

Night fell and Demeter lit a torch, stopping only long enough to watch it flare. In the dawn, the red flame of her torch burned thin and pale. The next day and night it burned, and the next, never extinguished by the rain or wind in the nine weary days and nights that Demeter searched the world over for Persephone.

On the tenth day, she happened to see another torch like her own, gleaming red in the mouth of a cave. Inside, on a heap of dry leaves, sat a woman whose dog-shaped head was crowned by a wreath of hissing snakes. It was Hecate, queen of the night, who never had a word to say to others unless they were as wretched as herself.

Demeter sat down on the dead leaves by Hecate's side.

"Oh Hecate," she moaned, "tell me, for pity's sake, have you seen my poor child, Persephone, pass by?"

"No," said Hecate in a cracked voice. "I've seen nothing of your daughter. But my ears hear cries of distress all over the world, and nine days ago, I heard the screams of a young girl. As well as I could judge, a dragon was carrying her away. I can tell you nothing more except that, in my opinion, you'll never see your daughter

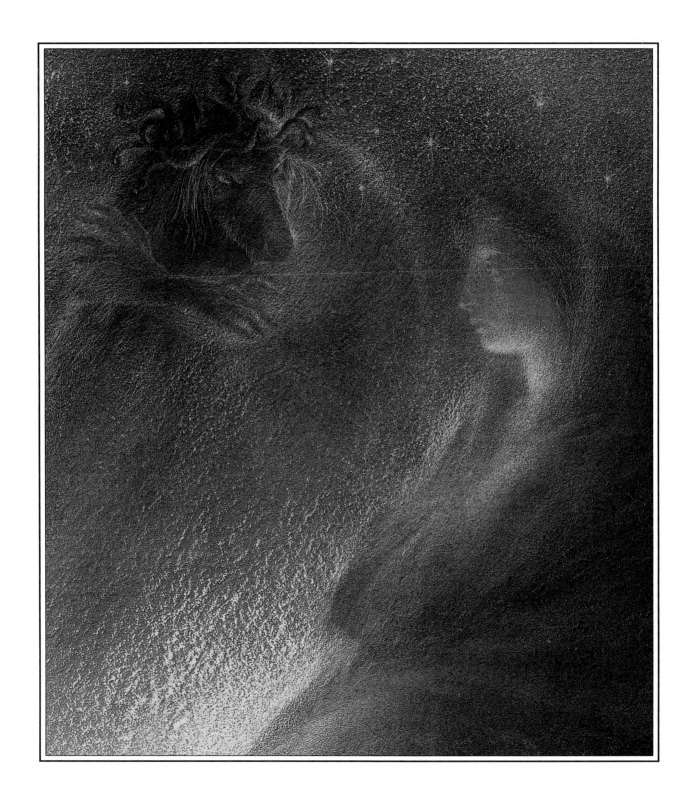

again. Stay here with me, and we will be the two most wretched women in the world."

"Not yet, dark Hecate," replied Demeter. "First come with your torch, and let us light the way together and look for her."

Hecate did not much like the idea of leaving her cave, even with someone as miserable as herself. "If it's light you're looking for, find Phoebus," she said, spitting into the sand. And she withdrew into a dark corner.

"Phoebus!" cried Demeter. And she made straight for the sunniest place in the world.

There she saw a beautiful young man with long golden ringlets made of sunbeams. His face was so radiant that Demeter had to hold her hands over her eyes for a moment. He was playing the lyre and singing a sweet song. As Demeter approached, Phoebus beamed at her, still singing.

"Phoebus," Demeter interrupted, "I have come to you for help. My daughter, Persephone, has disappeared."

"Persephone, Persephone," mused Phoebus. "Ah yes, a very

pretty girl. I'm happy to tell you, madam, that I did see her several days ago. She's safe and in excellent hands."

"You saw her?" cried Demeter, flinging herself at his feet. "Oh where is she?"

"As the girl was gathering flowers," said Phoebus (and as he spoke, he kept touching his lyre), "she was suddenly snatched by King Hades himself and carried off to his kingdom. I've never been to that part of the world, but the royal palace, I'm told, is built of gems. Gold, diamonds, and pearls will be your daughter's playthings. In spite of the lack of sunshine, she'll lead a very nice life."

"A very nice life!" echoed Demeter. "I've known my brother to be selfish. I've known him to be greedy. But I've never before known him to be heartless. My daughter is not a pretty gem he can pluck for his collection! Phoebus, will you light my way into Hades so I may demand that my wicked brother return Persephone to me?"

"To tell you the truth, I'm frightened of your brother's three-headed dog," Phoebus replied. "Cerebus would never let me pass

through the gates of Hades. Sunbeams are forbidden there, you know."

"Coward!" cried Demeter bitterly. "You have a harp instead of a heart. I will not sleep until I find the door to Hades, and when I do, let my brother beware!" And the high hills echoed her vow.

"Stay awhile," said Phoebus, pouting, "and let me turn the story of Persephone into verse."

But Demeter turned away, so filled with anger that she felt she could spread her arms and eclipse the sun.

Poor Demeter! All alone, never resting, never sleeping, holding her undying torch, she continued her search.

She suffered so much that, though she had been quite young when her troubles began, in a very short time she began to look old. She roamed about so wildly that people ran when they saw her coming. She gave no thought to seed time or to harvest. In fact, there was nothing in which she took an interest except children. When she saw them playing along the side of the road, she stood and stared at them with tears in her eyes, for she knew her greedy brother would do everything in his power to keep Persephone in the underworld.

In time, when she found no entrance to the underworld and was thwarted over and over again, she called upon her power to make things grow. Summoning all her strength, she came to a dreadful decision. Not a stalk of grain or a blade of grass, not a potato, or a turnip, or any other vegetable would grow until her daughter returned home. Not a single stalk of asparagus dared poke its spear out of the ground. She even forbade the flowers to bloom.

The farmers planted and plowed as usual, but the rich black soil lay as barren as a desert. The pastures turned brown. The rich man's acres and the poor man's patch were equally stricken. Even the children's flower beds showed nothing but dry stalks. The old people shook their heads and said the earth had aged like themselves. Cattle and sheep followed Demeter, lowing and bleating. But Demeter would not be moved.

"If the earth is ever to see grass again," she said, "it must grow along the green path my daughter walks coming home to me."

And she meant it.

Sounds of widespread weeping rose up to Mount Olympus. Loud prayers kept Zeus up all night. The king of the gods took a long look down to earth and saw the fields all blasted and parched. He saw thistles and brambles where before he had seen crops. He saw shriveled husks of corn and trees without their leaves.

And he saw Demeter, sitting grim and gray at the door of her empty home with her torch burning in her hand. Sighing, he took a look down into Hades to see how Persephone was faring.

Though she missed her mother every day and dreamed of her every night, Persephone was free to go wherever she wished in the underworld. She had found a number of ways to amuse herself. Behind King Hades' palace, she met a funny man named Sisyphus who was rolling a gigantic rock up a hill. When he reached the top, the rock would roll down and then he would start all over again.

And on the banks of the River Styx, she met forty-nine pretty girls filling forty-nine urns. The urns were full of holes so the water would run out, and the girls, called Danaides, were never done.

Persephone laughed at Sisyphus and she laughed at the Danaides but when she met Tantalus, she did not laugh. He was tied to a fruit tree bearing pears, apples, figs, and her favorites—pomegranates— but whenever the poor man tried to pick the fruit, a wind swept the branch away. He stood waist deep in a clear pool, but whenever he bent to drink, the water sank out of his reach, leaving the ground dry beneath his feet. Persephone watched him and wept, for she also longed for the taste of fresh fruit and water.

At night, Persephone dreamed of her golden-haired mother, in golden fields of ripening corn, dividing the grain from the chaff with a gust of wind. She dreamed of the sun baking the top of her head and the sweet smell of the soil and meadow grass. She dreamed of warm, ripe grapes and freshly baked bread. And some nights, she would wake in the dark castle and cry out, sick with hunger for home.

But when Zeus looked through the clouds, it was not the sad Persephone he saw. Desperate to please his captive, King Hades was on his knees before the beautiful girl while she taught him the game of jacks, only they were playing with rubies and diamonds. In Persephone's hair, King Hades had sprinkled flowers carved from precious gems, and she was wearing a dress of gold and silver thread that sparkled as she moved.

"Uncle," called Persephone, "let's play hide and seek now." And to Zeus's utter amazement, they did, using King Hades' prized and powerful helmet of invisibility. The helmet was so large, Persephone could hardly keep it balanced on her head, and her laughter gave away her hiding place. Then her uncle laughed too, a deep rusty laugh ending in a barking cough that seemed to come from some place in his chest.

"Persephone, I have a present for you, just look," he said. And he held out an exquisite crown of black pearls. "Put it on and sit on my ebony throne." But Persephone snatched the crown and threw it to the other side of the hall where it crashed against the wall.

"I don't care for crowns!" she cried.

"I wish you liked me a little better," said King Hades, sighing.

"You should have tried to make me like you before kidnapping me," Persephone answered. "The best thing you can do now is to let me go home. Then I might remember you sometimes and think that you were as kind as you knew how to be. And maybe, someday, I might come back to visit you."

"No, no," said King Hades, shaking his head. "I would not trust you for that. You're too fond of the sun and of gathering flowers and of your mother's cooking. You still have not touched a bite of food. Aren't you hungry, my dear? No? If you eat, I will give you another present. Oh, please don't frown at me."

"Your gifts please you, Uncle, but they do not please me. If you will not take me home, then show me a garden where I may plant things and watch them grow."

King Hades gazed at her sadly. Seeing the king, who did seem to love her in his selfish way, looking so grand and so melancholy all at once, Persephone softened and, for the first time, went up to him and put her hand in his. King Hades bent his dark, gloomy face down to hers, but Persephone shrank from his kiss.

King Hades began to pace up and down, his hands clasped behind his back, his head bowed. "A garden . . ." he murmured, "a garden." Then he brightened. "Come with me," he said, and led her through thick brambles to a clearing behind the palace. It was a damp place, completely hidden in shadows.

King Hades drew something from inside his robe. "Open your hand," he instructed, and she obeyed. Then into her open palm, he spilled some black seeds. She looked up at him inquiringly.

"Plant them and you'll find that your garden does not need the light of day," he said.

Then he snapped his fingers and a spirit appeared, a little boy with peculiar lidless eyes.

"You're new here in my kingdom," said King Hades to the child. "And I hear that you're good at gardening."

"Yes sir," replied the boy, staring at Persephone.

"Well then, you shall help my niece with her garden."

"Yes sir," the boy repeated, but he never looked at King Hades, only at Persephone.

King Hades put a hand on the boy's shoulder and bent down to whisper something into his ear. Then he left them to their work, and within an hour, the plot was covered with odd plants, the likes of which Persephone had never seen before.

Out of the ground sprouted black orchids, nightshade and mushrooms, henbane and hellebore. It was a strange assortment, but Persephone was happier than she had been since she had been snatched away, for like her mother she was making things grow.

Thinking of her mother, she was startled to have her thoughts interrupted by the boy. "I met your mother once," he said.

Persephone shook her head and laughed. "I'm sure you never met my mother," she said. Then she drew herself up haughtily, for the way the boy was looking at her with his strange eyes made her uncomfortable.

"Oh yes, I have," the boy insisted. "In fact, she changed me into a lizard . . ." He trailed off, shuddering. "If I hadn't met your mother, I wouldn't be here," he finished.

Persephone had been told that spirits took a while to adjust to the underworld and that their minds, even before drinking the waters of Lethe, often became confused. She decided that was what must be wrong with the boy.

He drew closer.

"There's a fruit tree that grows in King Hades' kingdom," he whispered. "You're hungry, aren't you? Come with me and I'll show it to you."

"I've seen the tree," she said. "It's there to tempt poor Tantalus."

"No," said the boy. "There's another. It's not far." He studied her face. Satisfied that she would follow, he marched through the garden into the undergrowth.

The path he cut through the thick vines and creepers grew murkier until all at once they came to a small clearing. A single tree stood in a grassy circle.

"Pomegranates!" whispered Persephone. They were so round and red, they made her feel faint. The boy walked up to the tree, moving as if he were under water. Slowly, he reached up and picked a pomegranate and, slowly, he brought it to his mouth.

"We're alone," he said. "No one will see us. No one will know." He cracked it open on a rock and began to eat juicily. Then he came toward her, smiling, his mouth smeared red with juice.

"Eat," he said.

She looked around. It was true. No one could see them in that secret spot. No one, that is, except Zeus—but Persephone had no idea that he was watching.

She took the fruit and with shaking fingers dug out the tiny tart seeds. One. Two. Three. She put them in her mouth and swallowed them. Nothing had ever tasted so delicious.

Just as Persephone ate the third seed, a high-pitched shout split the air and she dropped the pomegranate. Persephone recognized that call. It was Hermes, messenger of the gods, sent by Zeus from Mount Olympus! She ran as fast as she could to meet him.

Hermes put his arm around Persephone's waist and pulled her up into the air.

"Come away!" he cried. "Zeus has sent me to take you home."

Persephone had dreamed those words so many times that she thought maybe she was dreaming now.

"What about my uncle?" she asked. "We have to say good-bye."

"No time for good-byes," said Hermes, noticing her lips were red with juice. But to her surprise, Persephone was finding it hard to leave so suddenly. King Hades had been kind to her and, unlike her mother, he had allowed her to go wherever she pleased in his kingdom all by herself. She thought how lonely he would be without her and how dreary his palace would seem after she was gone. And hadn't he just given her a garden of her own? How could she run away without saying good-bye?

"Come," Hermes begged, wrapping his arm more tightly around her and lifting her higher. "Don't dawdle, Persephone. Zeus may change his mind."

Looking down, Persephone saw the lizard boy rush off with something red in his hand, yelling, "King Hades, King Hades!" When her uncle heard she had eaten the seeds, would he keep her in the underworld forever?

She shivered, suddenly afraid. "Take me home," she whispered.

Hermes guided her through the great gateway of Hades, leaving the three-headed Cerebus barking and growling like thunder behind them. When finally they emerged on the earth, Hermes bowed gracefully, and flew away before she could thank him.

Persephone took a deep breath. How she had missed the sweet familiar smells! The sun warmed her face as she hurried along, and the path turned green behind her. Violets and daisies sprang up along the wayside, and wherever she stepped, a flower grew.

Demeter was still sitting sadly on her doorstep, with her torch burning in her hand. She had been gazing into the flame when, all at once, it flickered and almost went out.

Lifting her head, she was surprised to see the sudden band of green stretching over the barren fields.

"Does the earth disobey me?" she exclaimed. "Is it turning green when I've commanded it to be barren until my daughter is safe in my arms?"

"Then open your arms, Mother," cried a familiar voice. And Persephone came running, and flung herself into her mother's arms.

Clinging to one another, they wept and wept.

At last, when their hearts had grown quiet, Demeter studied Persephone. "My child," she said, "did you taste the food of the dead while you were in King Hades' palace?"

"Until today, I had not one bite," answered Persephone. "But today, I met a strange boy who said you had changed him into a lizard. And, though he was a new spirit, he seemed to know his way in the underworld—almost as if Uncle Hades had shown him around himself! He led me to a pomegranate tree and . . . Oh Mother, I know I shouldn't have, but I was so hungry that I ate three seeds!"

When her daughter mentioned the lizard boy, her mother turned pale. "Ah, miserable me," she cried when Persephone had finished her story. "For each of those three pomegranate seeds, you must spend one month of every year in King Hades' palace in the underworld. Nine months with me and three with your wretched uncle!"

Demeter moaned. "But as long as you are there, my child, the earth will mourn with me. Nothing shall grow. And those cold months will be called winter."

Persephone kissed her mother and stroked her gray hair.

"I don't really mind spending three months with my uncle," she said, "if I can spend the other nine with you. Though he is the king of the dead, he loves me too, don't you think?"

Looking into Persephone's eyes, Demeter saw that her daughter had grown. When she left she had been a child, whose light step on the hillside made it bloom. Now, every spring, she would again make the hillsides bloom but always with the memory of the coming of winter when the earth would sleep under frost.

As Demeter thought about winter, the torch she had carried all those months, looking for her lost child, flickered one last time and went out. Drawing her arm back, Demeter threw it into the air with such force that it landed far away, instantly buried in the bright field of new flowers.

Then Demeter just stood there, looking out at the horizon.

Persephone gently took her hand. "Are you sad because someday soon I will leave you again?" she asked.

"Yes," said her mother. "And because you are no longer a child."

Persephone smiled, her lips still red from the juice of the pomegranate.

Silently, they sat close together, watching the new moon rise over the distant sea. Demeter heard the waves, hissing like the snakes on Hecate's head. "In my opinion, you will never see your daughter again," Hecate had said. But there was her daughter, sitting by her side, alive and more radiant than ever.

"All those months when I was away from you," said Persephone softly, breaking the silence, "you were still with me, Mother."

"And you with me," said her mother. And at long last, she too could smile.